PUMPKINS, PASTRIES, AND PROMISES

PUMPKINS, PASTRIES, AND PROMISES

COZY AUTUMN ROMANCE

ANN LAUREL

My Best Friend is a person who will give me a book
I have not read.

— ABRAHAM LINCOLN

CHAPTER ONE

Zofia

I trudged through the pumpkin patch, my boots sinking into the soft earth with each step. The crisp October air nipped at my cheeks, carrying the scent of fallen leaves and distant bonfires. I'd come here hoping to find inspiration for my latest pottery project, but my mind kept wandering back to the stack of unpaid bills waiting for me at the studio.

"Focus, Zofia," I muttered to myself, scanning the rows of orange globes. "You're here for the perfect pumpkin, not to wallow in self-pity."

As I reached for a round specimen, my hand collided with someone else's. I jerked back, startled, and found myself face-to-face with a familiar pair of warm brown eyes.

"Corbin?" I blurted out, heat rising to my cheeks. "What are you doing here?"

He grinned, that lopsided smile that always made my heart skip a beat. "Probably the same thing you are," he said, gesturing to the pumpkin we'd both tried to grab.

"Looking for the perfect canvas for my latest culinary masterpiece."

I raised an eyebrow, intrigued despite myself. "Let me guess. Pumpkin pie?"

Corbin clutched his chest in mock offense. "Zofia, you wound me. As if I'd be so pedestrian." He leaned in conspiratorially, lowering his voice. "I'm thinking pumpkin creme brûlée. With a maple bourbon caramel."

The idea made my mouth water, and I smiled. "Okay, that does sound pretty amazing."

"Tell you what," he said, straightening up. "Why don't we join forces? Two sets of eyes are better than one when it comes to pumpkin hunting."

I hesitated, glancing at my watch. I really should get back to the studio, try to salvage something from this creative dry spell. But there was something in Corbin's eager expression that made it hard to say no.

"Alright," I conceded. "But only because I'm curious about this fancy pumpkin dessert of yours."

We set off down the rows, chatting easily as we examined pumpkins. It was nice, and I enjoyed the company. I'd gotten so used to doing everything alone, both in my personal life and my business, that I'd forgotten how pleasant it could be to share an experience with someone else.

"So, how's the pottery business going?" Corbin asked as we inspected a particularly knobbly pumpkin.

I stiffened, my good mood evaporating. "Oh, you know," I said, trying to keep my voice light. "It has its ups and downs."

Corbin gave me a sidelong glance. "Sounds like it might be more downs than ups lately."

I sighed, running a hand through my hair. "Is it that obvious?"

He shrugged. "I've been there. Running a business isn't easy, especially when you're passionate about what you do."

"Yeah, well, passion doesn't pay the bills," I muttered, kicking at a clod of dirt.

Corbin was quiet for a moment, and I immediately regretted my outburst. The last thing I needed was pity from the cute baker, who probably had customers lining up around the block.

"You know," he said finally, "my grandfather used to say that the toughest times in business are like kneading dough. It's hard work, and sometimes you want to give up, but if you keep at it, eventually you'll have something beautiful."

I couldn't help but chuckle. "Does your family have a baking metaphor for everything?"

"Pretty much," he admitted with a grin. "But seriously, Zofia. What's really going on?"

Maybe it was the crisp autumn air, or the way the setting sun cast everything in a golden glow, but suddenly I wanted to open up. "It's just I thought by now I'd have it all figured out, you know? But every time I think I'm getting ahead, something else comes up. A kiln breaks down, or a big order falls through, or..."

"Or you hit a creative block?" Corbin finished gently.

I nodded, surprised at how accurately he'd pinpointed my struggle. "How did you know?"

He shrugged, a rueful smile playing on his lips. "Let's just say I've had my fair share of staring at a blank recipe book, wondering if I'll ever have another original idea again."

"How do you get past it?" I asked, genuinely curious.

Corbin bent down to examine another pumpkin, turning it over in his hands as he considered the question. "Sometimes, I try to remember why I started baking in the first place. Other times, I force myself to try something completely new, even if it's terrible." He straightened up, meeting my eyes. "And sometimes, I just need to step away for a while. Give myself permission to not create for a day or two."

I frowned. "But doesn't that feel like giving up?"

"Not at all," he said, shaking his head. "Think of it like letting clay rest before you work with it. Sometimes you need that time to recharge and come back stronger."

His words struck a chord in me, and I nodded slowly. "I never thought about it that way before."

We continued our pumpkin hunt, but now the conversation flowed more freely. I told Corbin about some of my wilder pottery ideas with the ones I'd been too afraid to try, and he shared stories of spectacular baking failures that had me doubled over with laughter.

As the sun dipped lower on the horizon, painting the sky in brilliant oranges and pinks, we finally found our perfect pumpkins. Mine was a deep, rich orange with a slightly flattened top and perfect for making into a unique serving bowl. Corbin's was rounder, with a thick stem that he claimed would make an excellent handle for his pie or crème brûlée, or whatever culinary magic he was planning.

We made our way to the checkout stand, both of us a little quieter now that our adventure was ending. As we waited in line, I stole glances at Corbin. The fading sunlight caught in his hair, giving him an almost ethereal glow. He must have sensed my gaze, because he turned to me with a soft smile.

"This was fun," he said. "We should do it again sometime."

My heart did a little flip, but I tamped down the feeling. "Yeah, maybe," I said noncommittally. "If I can find the time between trying to save my business and battling creative blocks."

Corbin's smile faltered for a moment, but then he brightened. "Hey, I have an idea. Why don't you come by the bakery tomorrow morning? I'll have a fresh batch of those pumpkin spice cinnamon rolls you liked so much, and maybe we can brainstorm some ideas for your pottery."

I hesitated. Part of me wanted to say yes immediately, to grab onto this lifeline of friendship and support that Corbin was offering. But another part, the part that had experienced betrayal in the past, restrained itself.

"I don't know, Corbin," I said slowly. "I appreciate the offer, but I'm not sure I'm ready to mix business and whatever this is."

He nodded, understanding in his eyes. "No pressure, Zofia. The offer stands whenever you're ready. And hey, even if you just want to come by for a coffee and some quiet time to sketch, my door's always open."

As we paid for our pumpkins and prepared to go our separate ways, Corbin pulled out his phone. "At least let me give you my number," he said. "In case you change your mind. Or if you ever need an emergency taste-tester for your latest pottery glaze."

I laughed despite myself. "I'm pretty sure my glazes aren't edible, Corbin."

"You never know," he said with a wink. "I'm always up for culinary adventures."

Before I could overthink it, I pulled out my phone, and we exchanged numbers. As I watched Corbin walk to his car, pumpkin tucked under one arm, I felt a mix of emotions swirling inside me. Hope, fear, excitement, uncertainty, and they all battled for dominance.

On the drive home, my mind raced with possibilities. Could Corbin's fresh perspective be just what I needed to jumpstart my creativity? Or was I setting myself up for disappointment by letting someone else into my carefully constructed world of independence?

As I pulled up to my studio, the *Closed* sign in the window seemed to mock me. I carried my pumpkin inside, setting it on my worktable. In the fading light, its orange skin seemed to glow, full of potential.

I ran my fingers over its surface, feeling the bumps and ridges. Suddenly, an idea formed in my mind. What if I created a series of serving bowls inspired by the textures of different pumpkins? I could experiment with glazes to mimic the various shades of orange and green.

Excited for the first time in weeks, I reached for my sketchbook. As I drew, my phone buzzed with a text. It was from Corbin:

Hope you made it home safely. Remember, sometimes the seeds of creativity are found in unexpected places. Looking forward to seeing what amazing things you create!

I stared at the message, my pencil hovering over the paper. Part of me wanted to text back immediately, to thank him for the encouragement and maybe even take him up on that brainstorming session. Another part whispered caution, reminding me of past hurts and the importance of standing on my own two feet.

With a deep breath, I set my phone aside and turned back to my sketch. I had work to do, ideas to explore. The question of Corbin and what role he might play in my life and my business could wait. For now, I had pumpkins to transform and pottery to create.

As I lost myself in the flow of sketching, I couldn't help but smile. Maybe Corbin was right. Maybe the seeds of creativity really exist in unexpected places like a chance encounter in a pumpkin patch on an autumn afternoon.

The studio grew dark around me as I worked, but I

barely noticed. For the first time in weeks, the ideas were flowing freely, each sketch leading to another. I incorporated not just the textures of pumpkins, but other autumn elements as well, with the veins of leaves, the rough bark of trees, the delicate latticework of bare branches against the sky.

It was well past midnight when I finally set down my pencil, my hand cramping, but my heart was full. I looked around the studio, at the scattered sketches and the pumpkin still sitting on my work table, and felt a surge of hope. Maybe this was the turning point I'd been waiting for.

As I gathered my things to head up to my apartment, my gaze fell on my phone. Corbin's message still glowed on the screen, unanswered. I picked it up, my thumb hovering over the reply button.

What would happen if I let him in, just a little? If I allowed myself to accept his offer of friendship and support? The thought was both thrilling and terrifying.

CHAPTER TWO

*C*orbin

I burst through the door of Zofia's pottery studio, a cardboard box clutched to my chest and flour dusting my apron. "Zofia! I'm so sorry, I think I've made a terrible—" My words died in my throat as I took in the scene before me.

Zofia stood at her potter's wheel, hands covered in clay, her hair pulled back in a messy bun. She looked up at me, her eyes wide with surprise, a smudge of clay across her cheek. The morning sunlight streaming through the windows caught the dust motes swirling around her, giving her an almost ethereal glow.

"Corbin?" she asked, her voice a mix of confusion and amusement. "What are you doing here?"

Heat crept up my neck as I suddenly realized how I must look, disheveled, covered in flour, and holding a package that clearly wasn't hers. "I, uh... I think I delivered this to the wrong address," I stammered, holding up the box. "It was supposed to go to the flower shop next door, but I was distracted and, well, here I am."

Zofia's lips quivered into a smile as she reached for a nearby towel to wipe her hands. "And you decided to personally deliver it to the right place? That's very dedicated of you."

I chuckled, trying to regain my composure. "Well, you know me. Customer service is our top priority at Carmichael's Bakery."

She raised an eyebrow. "Even when it's not your customer?"

"Especially then," I quipped, finally finding my footing in our familiar banter. "You never know when someone might decide they need a croissant to go with their pottery."

Zofia laughed, the sound filling the studio and making my heart do a little flip. "Well, since you're here," she said, gesturing to a stool near her workbench, "why don't you take a load off? I was just about to take a break anyway."

I hesitated, glancing at my watch. "I really should get this package next door."

"Come on back then," she coaxed, her eyes twinkling. "I've got some of that herbal tea you like. Besides, I want to hear all about how the great Corbin Carmichael, master baker, managed to mix up a simple delivery."

Unable to resist her invitation or her teasing smile, I delivered the package next door and came back, and made my way to the stool. As I sat, I took in the organized chaos of her studio. Half-finished pottery pieces lined the shelves, each one unique and beautiful in its own way. Sketches and color swatches covered a large bulletin board, and the air was thick with the earthy scent of clay.

"So," Zofia said, handing me a steaming mug of tea before settling onto her own stool, "spill. What's got the usually unflappable Corbin Carmichael so distracted he's delivering packages to the wrong address?"

I took a sip of tea, buying myself a moment to gather my thoughts. I'd been thinking about her, and about our conversation in the pumpkin patch, about the way her eyes lit up when she talked about her art. But I couldn't exactly tell her that.

"It's been a busy morning at the bakery," I said instead. "We're trying out some new fall recipes, and I've been up since four experimenting."

Zofia leaned forward, her interest piqued. "Ooh, anything good?"

I couldn't help but grin. "Well, I don't want to brag, but I think I've perfected a maple pecan Danish that might just change your life."

"Bold claim, Carmichael," she teased. "You know I'm going to hold you to that, right?"

"I wouldn't have it any other way," I replied, feeling a warmth in my chest that had nothing to do with the tea. "How about you? How's the pottery business going?"

Zofia's smile faltered slightly, and I immediately regretted asking. I knew she'd been struggling lately, and I didn't want to bring up painful subjects. But to my surprise, she brightened again almost immediately.

"Actually, it's been going pretty well," she said, gesturing to the cluttered workbench behind her. "Remember that pumpkin we found at the patch? It sparked this whole new line of autumn-inspired pieces. I've been working non-stop for the past week, and I think I might actually have something special here."

I felt a surge of pride and happiness for her. "Zofia, that's fantastic! I told you sometimes inspiration comes from unexpected places."

She rolled her eyes, but her smile was genuine. "Yeah, yeah, don't let it go to your head, baker boy. But, thank you.

For that day at the pumpkin patch. I think I really needed that push to try something new."

Our eyes met, and for a moment, the air between us seemed to crackle with unspoken possibilities. I leaned in slightly, drawn by some invisible force.

Then Zofia cleared her throat and looked away, breaking the spell. "So, um, what about you? Any big plans for the bakery?"

I blinked, trying to refocus. "Oh, uh, yeah, actually. We're thinking about expanding."

Her eyebrows shot up. "Expanding? That's huge, Corbin! What are you thinking?"

I ran a hand through my hair, suddenly feeling the weight of the decision. "Well, we've been doing really well with our specialty cakes and pastries. There's been talk of opening a second location, maybe in the next town over. It would mean a lot more work, but also a chance to reach new customers, try new things..."

"But?" Zofia prompted gently, clearly sensing my hesitation.

I sighed. "But it's a big risk. We'd need to hire more staff, invest in new equipment. And my dad's not entirely on board. He thinks we should stick with what we know, keep things small and manageable."

Zofia nodded thoughtfully. "And what do you think?"

I paused, realizing I hadn't really allowed myself to consider what I wanted. "I think we need to grow. The world is changing, and if we don't change with it, we'll get left behind. But I also understand my dad's concerns. The bakery has been our family for generations. It's more than just a business to us."

"Sounds like you're caught between tradition and inno-vation," Zofia mused. "I can relate to that. It's not easy to take risks when you're passionate about what you do."

I looked at her, struck by how well she understood. "Exactly. How do you balance it? Staying true to your art while also running a successful business?"

Zofia laughed, but there was a hint of self-deprecation in it. "Oh, I'm probably not the best person to ask about running a successful business. But I do know something about staying true to your art."

She stood up suddenly, her eyes bright with an idea. "Here, let me show you something."

I watched, intrigued, as she went to her potter's wheel and sat down. With practiced movements, she centered a lump of clay on the wheel and worked. Her hands moved with grace and purpose, shaping the clay as it spun.

"When I first started out," she said, her voice soft but clear over the hum of the wheel, "I was so focused on making what I thought would sell. I studied market trends, tried to copy popular styles. And you know what? My work was terrible."

The clay took shape under her skilled fingers, rising and curving into a delicate form. "It wasn't until I stopped trying to please everyone else and started making what felt true to me that things started to click. Sure, not everything sells, but the pieces that do are special. They mean something."

I found myself mesmerized, not just by the emerging pottery, but by Zofia herself. The way she lost herself in her work, the passion in her voice, was beautiful.

"I think," she continued, her eyes still focused on the clay, "that's the key to any creative business. Whether it's pottery or baking. You have to innovate, yes, but in a way that stays true to who you are and what you love. Otherwise, what's the point?"

As she spoke, the clay transformed into a graceful vase, its sides adorned with delicate, leaf-like patterns. With a few final touches, she lifted her hands away and looked up at me, her eyes shining.

"Wow," I breathed, genuinely impressed. "Zofia, that's amazing."

She blushed slightly, looking pleased. "Thanks. It's just a rough draft, but I think it has potential."

"Potential?" I exclaimed. "It's gorgeous! I can already imagine it filled with flowers, sitting in someone's home. It's like you've captured autumn itself."

Zofia's blush deepened, and she ducked her head. "You're too kind. But that's kind of what I was going for. I want people to look at my pieces and feel something, you know? To be reminded of a crisp fall day, or a cozy moment by the fire."

I nodded, understanding completely. "That's how I feel about baking. It's not just about making something that tastes good, though that's important too. It's about creating an experience, a memory."

Our eyes met again, and this time, neither of us looked away. I felt a connection forming between us, deeper than just friendship or mutual admiration. It was as if we truly saw each other for the first time.

"Corbin," Zofia said softly, "I think—"

The shrill ringing of my phone interrupted whatever she was about to say. I jumped, the spell broken, and fumbled to silence it.

"Shoot, I'm sorry," I muttered, glancing at the screen. "It's my dad. I should probably..."

Zofia nodded, her expression unreadable. "Of course. You should get back to the bakery. I've kept you long enough."

I stood, suddenly awkward. "Thanks for the tea, and the demonstration. It was really inspiring."

She smiled, but it didn't quite reach her eyes. "Anytime."

I didn't want to leave things like this with so much left unsaid. "Zofia, I—"

"Go on," she said gently. "Your dad's waiting. But maybe we could do this again sometime? I'd love to hear more about your expansion plans."

Relief flooded through me. "Yeah, I'd like that. How about dinner? Tomorrow night?"

Zofia's eyes widened slightly, and for a moment, I feared I'd overstepped. But then she nodded, a small smile playing at her lips. "Dinner sounds great. Text me the details?"

"Absolutely," I said, unable to keep the grin off my face. "I'll see you tomorrow, then."

As I left the studio, my heart was pounding. I'd come here by accident, but it felt like something important had just happened. Something that could change everything.

My phone buzzed again, reminding me of the real world waiting outside. With a deep breath, I answered it. "Hey, Dad. Sorry, I got a bit sidetracked with a delivery. I'm on my way back now."

Walking back to the bakery, my mind fought between thoughts of expansion plans and the memory of Zofia's hands shaping clay. I couldn't shake the feeling that my life was about to change in ways I couldn't yet imagine.

The bell above the bakery door chimed as I entered, and the familiar scents of sugar and spice enveloped me. My dad looked up from behind the counter, his brow furrowed.

"There you are," he said, his tone a mix of relief and exasperation. "Where have you been? We've got a line of customers and a dozen cakes to decorate before noon."

I quickly stashed the misdelivered package behind the

counter, making a mental note to drop it off at the flower shop later. "Sorry, Dad. I got a little distracted."

He raised an eyebrow, clearly sensing there was more to the story, but thankfully didn't press. "Well, you're here now. Wash up and get started on those cakes. We'll talk about the expansion plans later."

As I tied on a fresh apron and began piping delicate rosettes onto a birthday cake, my mind wandered back to Zofia's studio. To the way her eyes lit up when she talked about her art, the grace of her hands as she worked the clay. I thought about what she'd said about staying true to yourself while also innovating.

Maybe that was the key to the bakery's future, too. Growing and changing without losing sight of what made us special. It wouldn't be easy, but nothing worth doing ever was.

My phone buzzed in my pocket, and I snuck a glance at it when Dad wasn't looking. It was a text from Zofia:

Thanks for the unexpected visit. Looking forward to dinner tomorrow. Maybe you can bring some of that life-changing Danish? ;)

CHAPTER THREE

*Z*ofia

I pushed open the door to Carmichael's Bakery, a little bell chiming overhead to announce my arrival. The warm, yeasty scent of fresh bread enveloped me, mingling with the sweet aroma of cinnamon and vanilla. My stomach growled, reminding me I skipped lunch again in favor of finishing a new batch of mugs.

The bakery was bustling with afternoon customers, a line snaking its way to the counter where Corbin stood, effortlessly juggling orders and conversation. He glanced up as I entered, and his face broke into a wide grin that made my heart do a little flip.

"Zofia!" he called out, waving me over. "I was hoping you'd stop by today."

I made my way to the counter, weaving between tables filled with chattering patrons. "Hey, Corbin," I said, trying to keep my voice casual. "I thought I'd take you up on that offer to try your new Danish."

"Perfect timing," he said, his eyes twinkling. "I just pulled a fresh batch out of the oven." He turned to the display case, giving me a moment to admire the way his tee-shirt stretched across his shoulders as he bent to retrieve a pastry.

When he straightened up, he was holding a plate with a golden-brown Danish, still steaming slightly. The scent of maple and pecans wafted towards me, making my mouth water.

"Here you go," Corbin said, sliding the plate across the counter. "One life-changing Danish, as promised."

I raised an eyebrow, fighting back a smile. "Pretty confident in your baking skills, aren't you?"

He leaned in, lowering his voice conspiratorially. "Well, I did promise to change your life. I'd hate to disappoint."

A warmth that had nothing to do with the fresh pastry spread through my chest. I was acutely aware of how close we were, of the way Corbin's eyes crinkled at the corners when he smiled.

"Ahem," came a pointed cough from behind me. I turned to see an older woman giving us an amused look. "Don't mean to interrupt, dears, but some of us are here for the pastries, not the show."

The heat rushed to my cheeks as I quickly stepped aside. "Sorry," I mumbled, clutching my plate.

Corbin, ever the professional, seamlessly turned his attention to the waiting customer. "Mrs. Hendricks! Lovely to see you. The usual apple turnover today?"

As he chatted easily with Mrs. Hendricks, I found a small table near the window and sat down. I took a bite of the Danish, and my eyes widened. The pastry was perfectly flaky, the filling a harmonious blend of sweet maple and crunchy pecans. It was, I had to admit, pretty life-changing as far as pastries went.

I was so engrossed in my Danish that I didn't notice Corbin approaching until he slid into the chair across from me. "So," he said, a hint of nervousness in his voice, "what's the verdict?"

I made a show of consideration, tapping my chin thoughtfully. "Well, I don't know if my life has completely changed, but I might be ruined for all other pastries."

Corbin's face lit up. "I'll take it," he said with a chuckle. Then, leaning in slightly, he added, "You've got a little..." He gestured to the corner of his mouth.

Mortified, I quickly wiped at my mouth with a napkin. "Thanks," I said, feeling my cheeks heat again. "Guess I got a little carried away."

"Hey, no judgment here," Corbin said, holding up his hands. "I take it as a compliment. Besides," he added with a wink, "it's cute when you get enthusiastic about food."

I rolled my eyes, trying to ignore the flutter in my stomach at his words. "Careful, Carmichael. A girl might think you're flirting with her."

"And if I was?" he asked, his tone light but his eyes searching mine.

For a moment, I was at a loss for words. The air between us held a charged possibility. But before I could respond, the bell over the door chimed again, and a group of teenagers spilled into the bakery, their laughter breaking the spell.

Corbin glanced over his shoulder, then back at me with an apologetic smile. "Duty calls," he said, standing up. "But hey, before I go, I wanted to ask you something."

I nodded, curious. "Shoot."

"Well, you know the Harvest Festival is coming up next week," he began, running a hand through his hair. "I was wondering if maybe you'd like to go together? Not like a date or anything," he added quickly. "Just as friends. Or business associates. Whatever you're comfortable with."

My heart did a little somersault. The Harvest Festival

was Wintervale's biggest event of the year, a celebration of local artisans and businesses. I'd been planning to set up a booth to showcase my pottery, but the idea of experiencing it with Corbin was undeniably appealing.

"I'd like that," I said, surprised by how steady my voice sounded despite the butterflies in my stomach. "As friends," I added, not quite ready to put a label on whatever was developing between us.

Corbin's smile was bright enough to rival the afternoon sun streaming through the windows. "Great! It's a d- I mean, it's a plan." He glanced over at the growing line of customers. "I should get back to work, but maybe we could talk details later?"

I nodded, gathering my things. "Sounds good. I should head back to the studio anyway. Got a kiln full of mugs that need glazing."

As I stood to leave, Corbin surprised me by gently catching my wrist. "Wait," he said, "before you go, I wanted to show you something. Got a minute for a quick tour?"

Curiosity piqued, I nodded. "Sure, I guess I can spare a few minutes."

Corbin's face lit up. "Great! Hey, Dad," he called out to an older man I recognized as Mr. Carmichael, "can you watch the front for a bit? I'm going to show Zofia around."

Mr. Carmichael waved us off with a knowing smile that made me wonder just how obvious our mutual attraction was.

Corbin led me behind the counter, and through a swinging door into the bakery's kitchen. The space was a whirlwind of activity, with bakers kneading dough, decorating cakes, and sliding trays in and out of massive ovens.

"This is where the magic happens," Corbin said, his voice filled with pride. He guided me past gleaming stainless steel workstations, pointing out different areas. "Over there is where we do all our bread baking. And here," he said, stopping at a smaller station, "is where I work on developing new recipes."

I leaned in, examining the array of ingredients spread out on the counter. There were jars of spices, bottles of extracts, and bowls of fruits and nuts. It reminded me a bit of my workspace, with its collection of glazes and tools.

"It's amazing," I said, genuinely impressed. "I had no idea there was so much going on back here."

Corbin beamed at my interest. "Want to see something really cool?"

He led me to a small room off to the side of the main kitchen. As we entered, the temperature dropped noticeably, and I shivered slightly. Corbin noticed and moved closer, his warmth a stark contrast to the chilly air.

"This is our cold room," he explained. "It's where we store our more delicate creations."

I gasped as I took in the sight before me. Shelves lined the walls, filled with the most intricate and beautiful cakes and pastries I'd ever seen. There were tiered wedding cakes adorned with sugar flowers so lifelike I could almost smell their perfume, and delicate chocolate sculptures that looked like they'd shatter if you breathed on them too hard.

"Corbin," I breathed, "these are incredible. They're like... edible art."

He chuckled softly. "That's exactly how I see them. Each one is a little masterpiece, you know? Just like your pottery."

I turned to look at him, struck by the passion in his voice. In that moment, I saw Corbin not just as the charming baker who flirted with me over cinnamon rolls, but as a fellow artist, someone who understood the drive to create beauty.

"I never realized," I said softly. "I mean, I knew you were talented, but this... this is something else."

Corbin ducked his head, looking almost shy. "Thanks. It means a lot coming from you."

We stood there for a moment, surrounded by sugar and chocolate masterpieces, the air between us thick with unspoken feelings. I leaned in slightly, drawn by some invisible force.

Suddenly, a loud crash from the main kitchen broke the spell. We both jumped, then laughed nervously.

"We should probably head back," Corbin said, rubbing the back of his neck. "Before they send a search party."

As we made our way back through the kitchen, I couldn't help but feel like something had shifted between us. It wasn't just attraction anymore; there was a deeper understanding, a recognition of kindred spirits.

Back in the main bakery, the afternoon rush was in full swing. Corbin's dad gave us a knowing look as we emerged from the back, but thankfully, didn't comment.

"I should get going," I said, suddenly feeling a bit overwhelmed by the crowd and my own swirling emotions. "Thanks for the tour, and the Danish. It really was life-changing."

Corbin grinned. "Anytime. And hey, about the Harvest Festival, I was thinking maybe we could meet up the day before? Go over our booth setups, maybe grab dinner after?"

The idea sent a thrill through me, but I hesitated. "I don't know, Corbin. I've got a lot of work to do before the festival, and..."

"Come on," he coaxed, his eyes twinkling. "All work and no play makes Zofia a dull potter. Besides, I promise to feed you more life-changing pastries."

I couldn't help but laugh. "Well, when you put it like

that, how can I refuse? Okay, it's a date. I mean, not a date-date, just... you know what I mean."

Corbin's smile was soft. "I know exactly what you mean. I'll text you the details, okay?"

As I left the bakery, the little bell chiming behind me, my mind was a whirlwind of thoughts and emotions. The upcoming Harvest Festival, which had once seemed like just another business opportunity, now held the promise of something more. But as excited as I was, a nagging worry crept in. Could I balance my growing feelings for Corbin with my determination to make my business succeed on my own?

I glanced back through the bakery window, glimpsing Corbin chatting animatedly with a customer. He looked up, as if sensing my gaze, and gave me a quick wink before turning back to his work.

With a mix of anticipation and trepidation, I headed back to my studio. I had a lot of work to do before the festival, and even more to figure out about my feelings for a certain charming baker. As I walked, the taste of maple and pecans still lingering on my tongue, I couldn't shake the feeling that my life really had changed, Danish or no Danish.

The next few days passed in a blur of activity as I prepared for the Harvest Festival. My studio was a whirlwind of half-finished pieces, glaze samples, and packing materials. I'd focused on my new autumn-inspired line, hoping the seasonal theme would appeal to festival-goers.

Despite the hectic pace, my mind kept wandering back to Corbin and our upcoming not-date. We'd texted back and forth a few times, finalizing plans and exchanging the occasional bit of playful banter. Each message from him sent a little thrill through me, even as I tried to remind myself to keep things professional.

The day before the festival dawned crisp and clear, with just a hint of woodsmoke in the air. I spent the morning carefully packing my pottery into padded boxes, triple-checking my inventory list, and trying not to obsess over what to wear for dinner with Corbin.

As afternoon approached, I grew increasingly nervous. This wasn't just dinner with a cute guy; it was a chance to discuss our businesses, to maybe find ways to support each other professionally. But would our growing attraction complicate things?

I was so lost in thought that I nearly jumped out of my skin when my phone buzzed with a text from Corbin:

Hey, pottery queen! Ready for our pre-festival strategy session? I've got a table reserved at Bella's at 7. Can't wait to see you. :)

I smiled at the screen, warmth spreading through my chest. Taking a deep breath, I replied:

Looking forward to it, baker boy. See you soon!

As I hit send, I realized that despite my nerves, I was genuinely excited. Whatever happened between Corbin and me, I had a feeling it was going to be an interesting evening.

CHAPTER FOUR

*C*orbin

The Ferris wheel creaked to a stop, leaving Zofia and me suspended at the very top. The entire Harvest Festival sprawled out beneath us, a patchwork of twinkling lights and colorful booths. I grinned as I watched Zofia's eyes widen, taking in the view.

"Wow," she breathed, her breath visible in the crisp November air. "I've lived in Wintervale my whole life, but I've never seen it quite like this."

I chuckled, feeling a warmth in my chest that had nothing to do with the cup of mulled cider I'd been nursing. "Pretty amazing, right? It's like we're on top of the world up here."

Zofia turned to me, her cheeks flushed from the cold and maybe something more. "Thanks for convincing me to come up here, Corbin. I was worried about leaving our booths, but this is worth it."

I shrugged, trying to play it cool even as my heart did a little flip. "What can I say? I'm full of good ideas."

She rolled her eyes, but her smile was fond. "And so modest, too."

We lapsed into a comfortable silence, both of us taking in the scene below. The festival was in full swing, with locals and out-of-towners alike milling about, sampling food, playing games, and admiring the work of Wintervale's artisans. I could just make out our booths with my bakery's stand with its towering display of autumn-themed pastries, and Zofia's pottery booth next door, her new line of leaf-patterned mugs and bowls catching the light.

As I watched, I felt a surge of pride, not just for my own work but for Zofia's too. We'd spent the past week helping each other prepare, and seeing our booths side by side felt right somehow, like two pieces of a puzzle fitting together.

"Hey," I said softly, nudging Zofia's shoulder. "Look over there."

I pointed to where a small crowd had gathered around our booths. Even from this height, I could see people examining Zofia's pottery with interest, some already making purchases.

Zofia's face lit up. "Oh my, Corbin! It's working! People are actually buying my stuff!"

Without thinking, I reached out and squeezed her hand. "Of course they are. Your work is amazing, Zo. I told you it would be a hit."

She squeezed back, her eyes shining with a mix of excitement and what might have been unshed tears. "I couldn't have done it without you, you know. Your support, your ideas have made all the difference."

A lump formed in my throat. "Hey, that's what friends are for, right?"

Zofia's smile faltered for just a moment, and I wondered if

I'd said the wrong thing. Were we still just friends? The past week had been a whirlwind of shared meals, late-night texting sessions, and stolen glances across our adjoining booths. I'd been trying to take things slow, to respect Zofia's boundaries, but I couldn't deny the growing attraction between us.

Before I could overthink it, the Ferris wheel lurched back into motion, breaking the moment. As we descended, Zofia's hand slipped from mine, and I immediately missed its warmth.

Back on solid ground, we made our way through the festival, stopping to sample treats from other vendors and admire the handiwork of local artisans. I couldn't help but notice how Zofia seemed to gravitate closer to me as we walked, our hands brushing occasionally in a way that sent little sparks up my arm.

"Oh, look!" Zofia suddenly exclaimed, pointing to a booth decked out in autumn leaves. "Face painting! We should totally do that."

I raised an eyebrow. "Seriously? Aren't we a little old for face painting?"

She elbowed me playfully. "Come on, Corbin. Live a little! It'll be fun."

Unable to resist her enthusiasm, I let her drag me over to the booth. The artist, a teenager with bright blue hair, grinned at us. "What'll it be, folks? We've got fall leaves, pumpkins, scarecrows..."

"Ooh, I want a maple leaf!" Zofia said, settling into the chair. "What about you, Corbin?"

I hesitated, then shrugged. "Surprise me."

Ten minutes later, we emerged from the booth, Zofia sporting a delicate red and gold maple leaf on her cheek, while I had been adorned with an intricate, swirling pattern of autumn vines.

"You look adorable," Zofia said, reaching up to gently touch the design on my face.

I caught her hand, holding it against my cheek for a moment longer than necessary. "Right back at you."

We stood there for a moment, the sounds of the festival fading into the background as we gazed at each other. I found myself leaning in slightly, drawn by the warmth in Zofia's eyes and the soft curve of her smile.

"Zofia? Is that you?"

The moment shattered as Zofia jerked away, her eyes wide with what looked like panic. I turned to see a tall, well-dressed man approaching us, a look of surprise on his face.

"Marcus," Zofia said, her voice tight. "What are you doing here?"

The man, Marcus, smiled, but there was something cold about it that set my teeth on edge. "Can't a guy enjoy a small-town festival? I'm in the area on business and thought I'd stop by. It's been what, two years?"

Zofia nodded stiffly. "Something like that."

I cleared my throat, feeling the tension radiating off Zofia in waves. "Hi there, I'm Corbin," I said, extending my hand. "Corbin Carmichael."

Marcus shook my hand, his grip a little too firm. "Marcus Delacourt. I'm an old friend of Zofia's. We used to be business partners, actually."

The pieces suddenly clicked into place. This was the ex-partner Zofia had mentioned, the one who had betrayed her trust and nearly ruined her business. I felt a surge of protectiveness wash over me.

"Well, it's nice to meet you, Marcus," I said, keeping my tone polite but cool. "Zofia and I were just heading back to check on our booths. Lots of customers to attend to, you know how it is."

I placed a hand on the small of Zofia's back, ready to guide her away, but Marcus wasn't done.

"Booths? You mean you're still doing the pottery thing, Zo?" He chuckled, the sound grating on my nerves. "I thought for sure you'd have moved on to bigger and better things by now."

Zofia stiffened beside me. "Actually," she said, her voice stronger now, "my business is doing quite well. I've just launched a new line of autumn-inspired pieces that are selling like hotcakes."

Marcus raised an eyebrow. "Is that so? Well, good for you, I suppose. Though I can't help but wonder if you're really living up to your potential, stuck in this little town making mugs and bowls."

I'd had enough. "Hey, man," I said, stepping slightly in front of Zofia. "I don't know what your deal is, but Zofia's work is incredible. She's got talent and passion that you clearly couldn't appreciate. So why don't you just move along and enjoy the rest of the festival, alright?"

Marcus held up his hands in mock surrender. "No need to get defensive. I was just catching up with an old friend. But I can see when I'm not wanted." He turned to Zofia, his smile sharp. "It was good to see you, Zo. If you ever want to talk about opportunities, you know how to reach me."

With that, he melted back into the crowd, leaving Zofia and me standing there in stunned silence.

After a moment, I turned to Zofia, concern etched on my face. "Are you okay? That guy was a real piece of work."

Zofia nodded, but I could see she was shaken. "Yeah, I'm fine. I just wasn't expecting to see him here. It brought back a lot of bad memories."

I hesitated, then gently took her hand. "Do you want to talk about it? We could go somewhere quieter."

She seemed to consider it for a moment, then shook her head. "Not right now. I don't want to let him ruin our night. Can we just... I don't know, do something fun?"

"Absolutely," I said, giving her hand a squeeze. "How about we hit up the ring toss? I bet I can win you one of those giant stuffed pumpkins."

That got a small smile out of her. "Oh, you're on, Carmichael. But I warn you, I've got a mean throwing arm."

We made our way to the game booths, the encounter with Marcus still hanging over us like a cloud. But as we played game after game, I watched some of the tension leave Zofia's shoulders. She laughed as I spectacularly failed to knock down a pyramid of milk bottles, and cheered when she managed to land a ring around a bottle neck.

An hour later, we were laden down with an assortment of small prizes, no giant pumpkin, but Zofia was clutching a small stuffed black cat I'd won her, while I proudly wore a plastic crown from the *guess your weight* booth.

As we walked, I noticed Zofia shiver slightly in the cooling night air. Without a word, I shrugged off my jacket and draped it over her shoulders.

She looked up at me, surprised and something softer in her eyes. "Thanks," she said quietly. "You didn't have to do that."

I shrugged, trying to ignore the way my heart raced at her grateful smile. "Couldn't let you freeze. Besides, it looks better on you anyway."

Zofia rolled her eyes, but snuggled into the jacket. After a moment, she spoke again, her voice hesitant. "Corbin? About earlier, with Marcus..."

I nodded, encouraging her to continue.

She took a deep breath. "He wasn't just my business partner. We were involved. Romantically, I mean. I thought we were building something together, both in business and personally. But it turned out he was just using me to get to my designs. He took everything, my ideas, my client list, even some of my personal savings. Left me with nothing but debt and a broken heart."

My fists clenched at my sides. "Zofia, I'm so sorry. That guy's a real jerk."

She nodded, her eyes distant. "It took me a long time to trust anyone again after that. To believe in myself and my work. That's why I've been so hesitant about, well, us."

My heart skipped a beat. "Us?"

Zofia met my gaze, a mix of vulnerability and determination in her eyes. "Yeah, us. I like you, Corbin. A lot. But I'm scared. Scared of getting hurt again, scared of losing myself in someone else's dreams."

I took her hand, my thumb tracing gentle circles on her palm. "Zofia, listen to me. What happened with Marcus was awful, and you didn't deserve any of it. But I'm not him. I would never try to change you or take advantage of your talent. I think you're amazing just as you are with your creativity, your determination, even your stubbornness."

She let out a watery laugh at that.

I continued, my voice soft but earnest. "I don't want to pressure you into anything you're not ready for. But I want you to know that I'm here, whatever you need. Whether that's a friend, a business partner, or something more."

Zofia's eyes shimmered with unshed tears, but she was smiling. "How did I get so lucky to find someone like you?"

Before I could respond, a loud boom echoed through the air, making us both jump. We looked up to see the night sky explode with color as the festival's fireworks display had begun.

Without a word, I tugged Zofia over to a nearby hill where we could get a better view. We sat down on the grass, our shoulders touching, and watched as the sky lit up with bursts of red, gold, and green.

As a particularly spectacular explosion lit up the night, Zofia's hand slipped into mine. I looked over at her, the fireworks reflected in her eyes, and felt my breath catch in my throat.

"Corbin?" she said softly, barely audible over the booming fireworks.

"Yeah?"

She turned to face me, her expression a mix of nervousness and determination. "I think I'm ready to take a chance on us. If you still want to, that is."

My heart soared. "Are you kidding? Of course I do."

Slowly, giving her plenty of time to pull away if she wanted, I leaned in. Zofia met me halfway, her lips soft and warm against mine. The kiss was gentle, tentative at first, but quickly deepened as we both poured weeks of pent-up emotion into it.

When we finally pulled apart, both a little breathless, I rested my forehead against hers.

We settled back to watch the rest of the fireworks, Zofia tucked against my side, her head on my shoulder. As the final explosions lit up the sky, I couldn't help but feel like this was the start of something amazing.

But even as I reveled in the warmth of Zofia beside me, a nagging worry tugged at the back of my mind. Marcus's appearance had clearly shaken her, bringing up old wounds and insecurities. And something about the way he'd talked about *opportunities* made me uneasy. Would Zofia's past continue to haunt our budding relationship? And what if Marcus wasn't done causing trouble?

As the last echoes of the fireworks faded and the festival-goers began to disperse, Zofia and I lingered on our hillside perch, neither of us quite ready to break the spell of the evening.

"We should probably head back," Zofia said eventually, though she made no move to get up. "Check on our booths, start packing up."

I nodded, but tightened my arm around her slightly. "Yeah, probably. But maybe just five more minutes?"

She laughed softly, snuggling closer. "Okay, five more minutes."

We sat in comfortable silence, watching as the festival grounds slowly emptied, the twinkling lights being switched off one by one. It was like watching a dream fade away, but I didn't feel sad. The magic of the night wasn't ending; it was just changing form, settling into something warm and real between Zofia and me.

Finally, with a reluctant sigh, we stood up. I offered Zofia my hand, which she took with a smile that made my heart skip. As we made our way back down to the festival grounds, our fingers remained intertwined.

"So," I said, swinging our joined hands slightly, "what do you say we grab some coffee after we're done packing up? I know this great little 24-hour diner just outside of town."

Zofia raised an eyebrow. "Coffee? At this hour? Are you trying to keep me up all night, Carmichael?"

I felt heat rise to my cheeks. "What? No! I mean, not that I would mind staying up all night with you, but I didn't mean... I just thought..."

She laughed, squeezing my hand. "Relax, Corbin. I'm just teasing. Coffee sounds great."

I let out a relieved chuckle. "You're going to be trouble, aren't you?"

"You have no idea," she replied with a wink.

As we approached our booths, I was pleased to see that both had done well. My pastry display was nearly empty, with just a few straggling items left. Zofia's pottery booth looked equally successful, with many of her new autumn pieces sold.

"Looks like we both had a good night," I said, surveying the scene.

Zofia nodded, her eyes shining with pride. "I can't believe it. I've never sold this much at a festival before."

I bumped her shoulder playfully. "Told you people would love your work. You just needed to believe in yourself."

She turned to me, her expression soft. "Having you believe in me helped a lot, too."

We shared a smile, and I was just about to lean in for another kiss when a voice cut through the moment.

"Well, well. Isn't this cozy?"

We both turned to see Marcus standing there, his arms crossed and a smirk on his face. Zofia tensed beside me.

"Marcus," she said, her voice tight. "I thought you'd left."

He shrugged, sauntering closer. "I was on my way out when I realized we didn't really get a chance to catch up earlier. Thought I'd swing by and see how your little venture was doing."

I stepped forward slightly, positioning myself between Zofia and Marcus. "As you can see, it's doing great. Now, if you'll excuse us, we've got some packing up to do."

Marcus held up his hands in a placating gesture, but his eyes were cold. "No need to be hostile, baker boy. I'm just looking out for an old friend." He turned his attention to Zofia. "You know, Zo, my offer still stands. I've got connections in the city, galleries that would love to showcase your work. You could be making real money, not just peddling tchotchkes at small-town festivals."

My temper rose, but before I could say anything, Zofia spoke up.

"Thanks, but no thanks, Marcus," she said, her voice steady. "I'm doing just fine on my own. My *tchotchkes* as you call them, are selling well, and I've got plans to expand my online presence. I don't need your connections or your backhanded compliments."

Marcus's smirk faltered for a moment before returning full force. "Come on, Zofia. Don't let your pride get in the way of a good opportunity. You and I, we made a great team once. We could do it again, bigger and better this time."

I couldn't stay silent any longer. "I think she made herself clear, man. She's not interested."

Marcus's eyes flashed with anger. "Stay out of this, Carmichael. This is between me and Zofia."

"No, it's not," Zofia said firmly, stepping up beside me and taking my hand. "Corbin's right. I'm not interested in your offer, Marcus. What we had is in the past, and that's where it's going to stay. I've moved on, and I suggest you do the same."

For a moment, Marcus looked genuinely taken aback. Then his expression hardened. "Fine. Have it your way. But don't come crying to me when this little small-town romance fizzles out and you're left with nothing but a bunch of unsold pottery and broken dreams."

With that, he turned on his heel and stalked off into the night.

As soon as he was out of sight, Zofia let out a shaky breath. I immediately pulled her into a hug, feeling her tremble slightly against me.

"Hey, you okay?" I asked softly, running a hand up and down her back.

She nodded against my chest. "Yeah, I think so. That was intense."

I pulled back slightly to look at her. "You were amazing, Zo. The way you stood up to him? That took guts."

A small smile played on her lips. "It felt good, actually. Like I was finally closing that chapter of my life for good."

I brushed a strand of hair from her face, marveling at her strength. "I'm proud of you. And for what it's worth, I don't think this is just some small-town romance that's going to fizzle out."

Zofia's smile widened. "Me neither. But maybe we should take things one step at a time. Starting with that coffee you promised me?"

I grinned, feeling a weight lift off my shoulders. "Absolutely. Let's get this stuff packed up and hit the road. I've got a feeling we've got a lot to talk about."

As we worked side by side to dismantle our booths, I felt a mix of excitement and trepidation about what the future held. Zofia and I were just starting out, and there were bound to be challenges ahead. Marcus's reappearance had shown that the past had a way of cropping up when you least expected it.

But looking at Zofia, her face flushed with exertion and a determined set to her jaw, I knew we could handle whatever came our way. We were both artists at heart, used to taking raw materials and shaping them into something beautiful. Our relationship might be new and a little rough around the edges, but I had a feeling that with time and care, we could create something truly spectacular together.

As we loaded the last box into my truck, Zofia turned to me with a mischievous glint in her eye. "Race you to the diner? Loser buys the coffee."

I laughed, feeling lighter than I had in years. "You're on, pottery queen. But don't say I didn't warn you, I've got a mean lead foot."

With that, we jumped into our respective vehicles, the

night air filled with the sound of revving engines and our laughter.

CHAPTER FIVE

Zofia

I pulled my car into the gravel driveway, the crunch of stones under my tires mingling with the distant sound of laughter and crackling flames. My heart did a little flip as I spotted Corbin's truck already parked among the cluster of vehicles. He was here.

Taking a deep breath, I checked my reflection in the rearview mirror. My cheeks were flushed, whether from excitement or the crisp November air, I couldn't tell. I ran a hand through my wavy blonde hair, trying to tame the windblown strands, then grabbed the container of home-made s'mores dip from the passenger seat.

As I rounded the corner of the house, the bonfire came into view. It was a picturesque scene, straight out of an autumn-themed rom-com. A group of about a dozen people gathered around the roaring fire, some perched on logs, others sprawled out on blankets. The flames cast a warm, flickering light over everything, making the entire world seem softer somehow.

And there, leaning against a tree with a red solo cup in

hand, was Corbin. He looked up as I approached, his face breaking into a smile that made my knees go a little weak. God, would I ever get used to that?

"Zofia!" he called out, pushing off from the tree and making his way towards me. "You made it!"

I grinned, holding up the container. "Wouldn't miss it. I brought reinforcements."

Corbin peered at the dish, his eyes lighting up. "Is that your famous s'mores dip?"

"Maybe," I teased. "You'll have to stick around to find out."

He placed a hand over his heart in mock offense. "As if I'd be anywhere else."

We made our way to the fire, where Corbin introduced me to a few people I didn't know, friends from the bakery, and some of his old high school buddies. I settled onto a log, Corbin right beside me, our thighs just barely touching.

As the night wore on, I relaxed more and more. The conversation flowed easily, punctuated by bursts of laughter and the occasional pop from the fire. I watched, amused, as Corbin regaled the group with the story of how he'd once accidentally used salt instead of sugar in a batch of cookies at the bakery.

"I'm telling you," he said, gesturing wildly, "I've never seen my dad's face turn that shade of purple before. I thought he was gonna burst a blood vessel!"

Everyone erupted in laughter, and I joined in, caught up in Corbin's infectious enthusiasm. As our chuckles died down, he turned to me, his eyes twinkling in the firelight.

"Alright, Zo, your turn. What's your most embarrassing pottery mishap?"

A blush crept up my cheeks, partly from the nickname he'd never called me that before, and partly from the memory that immediately sprang to mind.

"Oh god," I groaned, covering my face with my hands. "Do I have to?"

"Come on," Corbin coaxed, gently pulling my hands away. "It can't be worse than the salt cookie incident."

I sighed dramatically, but couldn't keep the smile off my face. "Fine. But you asked for it." I turned to address the group. "So, picture this: I'm in my first year of art school, and we're doing a wheel-throwing demonstration for some potential students..."

As I launched into the tale of my spectacular pottery fail, involving a wheel spinning way too fast, clay flying everywhere, and me ending up looking like a mud monster, Corbin kept his eyes on me, never leaving my face, and there was a softness in his expression that made my heart race.

When I finished my story, everyone was in stitches, and I felt a warm glow of pride. It felt good to make people laugh, to be part of this easy camaraderie.

As the laughter died down, I suddenly realized how chilly the night had become. A shiver ran through me, and I rubbed my arms, wishing I'd thought to bring a heavier jacket.

Without a word, Corbin shrugged off his own jacket, a worn leather number that smelled faintly of cinnamon and yeast, and draped it over my shoulders.

"Oh, you don't have to," I said, but he cut me off with a gentle smile.

"I want to," he said softly, his hand lingering on my shoulder for a moment longer than necessary. "Can't have my favorite potter turning into a popsicle, can I?"

I ducked my head, hoping the firelight would hide my blush. "Thanks," I murmured, pulling the jacket tighter around me. It was still warm from his body, and I found myself surrounded by his scent.

As the night wore on, people drifted away in twos and threes. Soon, it was just Corbin and me, along with a couple of his friends, who were deep in conversation on the other side of the fire.

"Hey," Corbin said, nudging my shoulder gently. "Want to take a little walk? I brought some hot cocoa in a thermos."

My heart skipped a beat. "That sounds perfect."

We stood up, and Corbin grabbed a plaid blanket from the pile near the fire. As we walked away from the bonfire, a mix of nervousness and excitement bubbled up inside me. We'd been dancing around this thing between us for weeks now, neither quite ready to take that final step. But tonight felt different somehow.

Corbin led me to a small clearing close to the fire. The flames were still visible, casting a warm glow through the trees, but we were far enough away that conversation wouldn't carry. He spread out the blanket and we sat down, our shoulders touching.

"So," he said, pouring steaming cocoa into two mugs. "How's the pottery business going? I noticed you've been pretty busy lately."

I took a sip of the cocoa, savoring the rich chocolate flavor. "It's been amazing, actually. Remember those pottery classes I started offering last month?"

Corbin nodded, his eyes bright with interest.

"Well, they've really taken off," I continued, unable to keep the excitement out of my voice. "I'm booked solid for the next two months, and I've even had to start a waiting list."

"Zo, that's incredible!" Corbin exclaimed, giving my knee a squeeze. "I knew you could do it."

A warmth spread through me that had nothing to do

with the cocoa. "Thanks. It feels good, you know? Like I'm finally starting to build something real."

Corbin's smile was soft in the dim light. "I'm really proud of you. You've come so far since... well, since everything with Marcus."

I tensed slightly at the mention of my ex, but to my surprise, the usual ache that accompanied thoughts of him was barely there. Instead, I focused on the man beside me, on his unwavering support and belief in me.

"I couldn't have done it without you," I said softly, meeting his gaze. "Your encouragement, your friendship means everything to me."

He set his mug down, turning to face me fully. "Zofia, I-" he started, then paused, seeming to gather his thoughts. "These past few months, getting to know you, watching you chase your dreams has been incredible. You're incredible."

My breath caught in my throat. "Corbin..."

He reached out, gently tucking a strand of hair behind my ear. His hand lingered on my cheek, and I leaned into his touch.

"I know we said we'd take things slow," he murmured, his voice low and husky. "And if you're not ready, that's okay. But Zo, I can't pretend anymore. I'm falling for you. Hard."

Time seemed to stand still. The crackling of the distant fire, the rustle of leaves in the breeze, even my heartbeat, everything faded away until there was nothing but Corbin's warm brown eyes and the feel of his hand on my face.

"I'm falling for you too," I whispered, surprised by how easily the words came. "I think I have been for a while now."

Corbin's smile was brighter than the bonfire. Slowly, giving me plenty of time to pull away if I wanted to, he leaned in. I met him halfway, my eyes fluttering closed as our lips finally met.

The kiss was soft at first, tentative, like we were both afraid the other might disappear if we pushed too hard. But then Corbin's arm slipped around my waist, pulling me closer, and something inside me ignited.

I wound my arms around his neck, deepening the kiss. He tasted like chocolate, and I got lost in the sensation. All the tension, all the dancing around each other we'd been doing for weeks, all came pouring out in that kiss.

When we finally pulled apart, both a little breathless, Corbin rested his forehead against mine.

We stayed like that for a moment, just breathing each other in. Then Corbin pulled back slightly, his expression suddenly serious.

"Zofia," he said, taking my hands in his. "I want you to know that this isn't just some fling for me. I'm in this, all in, if that's what you want. But I also understand if you need more time, or if-"

I cut him off with another quick kiss. "Corbin, stop. I'm all in too. I know we've both got baggage, and there's still a lot we need to figure out. But I want to figure it out together."

The smile that broke across his face was like the sun coming out from behind the clouds. He pulled me into a tight hug, and I melted against him, feeling safer and more content than I had in years.

As we sat there, wrapped in each other's arms with the sounds of the dying bonfire in the background, I couldn't help but marvel at how much had changed in just a few short months. I'd gone from a struggling artist, afraid to trust anyone, to this with a growing business, newfound confidence, and a man who looked at me like I hung the moon.

But even as I reveled in the moment's warmth, a small voice in the back of my mind whispered a warning. Things were going so well, almost too well. What if it all came crashing down? What if I wasn't ready for this after all?

I pushed the thoughts aside, determined not to let my old fears ruin this perfect moment. For now, I was content to stay right here, wrapped in his arms and the scent of wood smoke, looking forward to whatever the future might bring.

As the night grew later and the bonfire dwindled to embers, Corbin and I reluctantly decided it was time to head home. We walked back to the parking area hand in hand, stealing glances at each other like lovesick teenagers.

"So," Corbin said as we reached my car, his thumb tracing circles on the back of my hand. "What are you doing tomorrow?"

I pretended to think for a moment. "Oh, you know, just the usual. Throwing some pots, maybe glazing a few pieces. Why do you ask?"

He grinned, pulling me closer. "Well, I was thinking maybe you could pencil me in for lunch? I know this great little café that just opened up downtown."

"Hmm, I don't know," I teased. "My schedule's pretty packed. But I suppose I could squeeze you in."

Corbin's laugh was low and warm. "How generous of you."

He leaned in for another kiss, and I met him eagerly. This one differed from our first as less tentative, more sure. It held the promise of many more kisses to come, and I lost myself in the sensation.

When we finally broke apart, I was a little dazed. "Okay, yeah," I said breathlessly. "Lunch tomorrow sounds great."

Corbin's smile was soft and a little smug. "Great. I'll pick you up at noon?"

I nodded, not trusting my voice. With one last quick peck, Corbin headed to his truck, looking back to wave before he climbed in.

As I watched his taillights disappear down the road, I leaned against my car, my head spinning. So much had changed in just one night. Corbin and I had crossed a line, one we couldn't uncross. And while part of me was thrilled, another part was terrified.

What did this mean for our friendship? For our businesses? We'd been such good friends and supporters of each other's work. What if a romantic relationship complicated all of that?

And then there was the bigger fear, the one I'd been trying to ignore all night. What if I wasn't ready for this? What if my past with Marcus had damaged me more than I realized?

As I drove home, my mind raced with possibilities, both good and bad. By the time I crawled into bed, I was a mix of excitement and anxiety. I tossed and turned for hours, replaying every moment of the night in my head.

It was nearly dawn when I finally drifted off, Corbin's jacket still draped over my chair, its familiar scent a comforting presence in the quiet of my bedroom. My last conscious thought was a hope that tomorrow's lunch date would help settle the butterflies in my stomach, or at least, that Corbin's smile would make them worth it.

CHAPTER SIX

*C*orbin

I burst through the door of Zofia's pottery studio, my heart pounding in my chest. The bell above the door jangled wildly, startling Zofia, as she hunched over her potter's wheel.

"Corbin?" she asked, her brow furrowed with concern. "What's wrong?"

I took a deep breath, trying to calm myself. "Zo, we've got a problem. A big one."

She stood up, wiping her clay-covered hands on her apron. "What is it?"

I ran a hand through my hair, frustration bubbling up inside me. "I just overheard Mrs. Pendleton at the bakery. She was telling everyone that your pottery contains lead and that it's not safe to use."

Zofia's face paled. "What? That's ridiculous! I would never use lead glazes. Where did she even get that idea?"

I shook my head, anger rising in my chest. "I don't know, but it's not just her. There are rumors all over town.

People are saying your clay isn't food-safe, that your glazes contain harmful chemicals. It's a mess, Zo."

She sank back onto her stool, looking shell-shocked. "This can't be happening. I've worked so hard to build my reputation. If people believe these rumors..."

I knelt beside her, taking her hands in mine. "Hey, we're not going to let that happen, okay?"

Zofia nodded, but I could see the worry etched on her face. "But how? If people are already talking..."

"We fight back with the truth," I said firmly. "We'll show them your certifications, explain your process. Hell, we'll invite them to watch you work if we have to."

A small smile tugged at the corners of her mouth. "You really think that'll work?"

I squeezed her hands. "I know it will. People in this town know you. They trust you. We just need to remind them why."

She took a deep breath, some of the tension leaving her shoulders. "Okay. What's our first move?"

I stood up, my mind already racing with ideas. "First, we need to find out where these rumors are coming from. Then we tackle them head-on."

We spent the next hour strategizing, mapping out a plan of action on the back of some old pottery sketches. As we worked, I marveled at Zofia's resilience. Despite the shock and stress, she was already bouncing back, her creative mind coming up with solutions I never would have thought of.

"What if we host an open house?" she suggested, her eyes lighting up. "We could invite people to come see the studio, explain the glazing process, maybe even let them try throwing a pot themselves?"

I grinned, feeling a surge of pride. "That's brilliant, Zo.

We could make it a whole event. I'll bring some pastries from the bakery, make it a real community thing."

She nodded enthusiastically, then paused, her expression growing serious. "Corbin, thank you. For being here, for helping me through this. I don't know what I'd do without you."

I pulled her into a hug, breathing in the familiar scent of clay and lavender that always clung to her. "Hey, that's what partners are for, right?"

As we broke apart, I saw a flash of something in Zofia's eyes, something that made my heart skip a beat. But before I could dwell on it, my phone buzzed in my pocket.

I glanced at the screen and frowned. "It's my dad. Apparently, there's some kind of commotion at the bakery. I should probably head back."

Zofia nodded, concern creasing her brow. "Go. I'll start working on flyers for the open house."

I hesitated at the door, not wanting to leave her alone. "You sure you'll be okay?"

She gave me a small smile. "I'll be fine. Go save the bakery."

With one last look at Zofia, I hurried out the door and down the street towards Carmichael's Bakery. As I approached, I could see a small crowd gathered outside, their voices raised in agitation.

I pushed my way through, my stomach dropping as I caught snippets of conversation.

"...heard they use expired ingredients..."

"...making people sick..."

"...health department should shut them down..."

I burst into the bakery to find my dad, red-faced and flustered, trying to calm an irate customer.

"I'm telling you, there's nothing wrong with our food!"

Dad insisted. "We've been serving this community for three generations!"

I stepped in, placing a hand on Dad's shoulder. "What's going on here?"

The customer, a middle-aged woman I recognized as a regular, turned to me with fire in her eyes. "I'll tell you what's going on. My whole family got sick after eating your cinnamon rolls last week. And now I hear you're using cheap, expired ingredients to cut costs!"

It felt like they punched me in the gut. "Mrs. Hawkins, I can assure you that's not true. We would never compromise on quality or safety."

But Mrs. Hawkins wasn't having it. "Save it, Corbin. I thought I could trust you folks, but clearly, I was wrong."

As she stormed out, I turned to my dad, my mind reeling. "What the hell is happening?"

Dad shook his head, looking more defeated than I'd ever seen him. "I don't know, son. But these rumors are spreading like wildfire. If we don't do something fast, we're going to lose everything."

I took a deep breath, trying to think clearly through the panic threatening to overwhelm me. "Okay, here's what we're going to do. First, we need to address these rumors head-on. Let's post our health inspection records in the window, maybe even invite the health department to do another inspection right now."

Dad nodded, some of the fight coming back into his eyes. "Good idea. What else?"

"We'll offer free samples," I continued, the plan forming as I spoke. "Let people taste for themselves that our food is fresh and delicious. And we'll be completely transparent about our ingredients and processes."

As we worked to implement our plan, my mind kept drifting back to Zofia. The timing of these attacks on both our businesses couldn't be a coincidence. Someone was deliberately trying to sabotage us, but who? And why?

By late afternoon, we'd calmed most of our customers' fears. The health inspector had given us a clean bill of health, and the free samples had reminded people why they loved our baked goods.

As the last customer left, clutching a bag of apology cookies, I slumped against the counter, exhaustion washing over me.

"You did good today, son," Dad said, patting me on the back. "I don't know what we would have done without you."

I managed a weak smile. "Thanks, Dad. But we're not out of the woods yet. We need to figure out where these rumors are coming from."

Just then, the bell above the door chimed. I looked up to see Zofia rushing in, her face flushed and her eyes wide.

"Corbin! I think I know who's behind all this!"

I straightened up, instantly alert. "What? Who?"

Zofia took a deep breath. "I was at the grocery store, picking up supplies for the open house, when I overheard Gloria Simmons talking to her friend. She was bragging about how she was going to run us both out of business."

My fists clenched at my sides. Gloria Simmons, owner of the new bakery that had opened across town a few months ago. I'd always thought her overly competitive, but this? This was crossing a line.

"I'm going to have a little chat with Ms. Simmons," I growled, already heading for the door.

Zofia caught my arm. "Corbin, wait. We need to be smart about this. If we confront her without proof, she'll just deny everything."

I knew she was right, but the anger coursing through me made it hard to think rationally. "So what do we do?"

Zofia's eyes gleamed with determination. "We gather evidence. And then we show everyone in town exactly who Gloria Simmons really is."

As we huddled together, planning, I had a surge of admiration for Zofia. Despite everything she'd been through today, she was still fighting, still strategizing. It made me realize something I think I'd known for a while but had been too afraid to admit.

I was in love with her.

The realization hit me like a ton of bricks, nearly knocking the wind out of me. But as I looked at Zofia, her face animated as she outlined her ideas. I knew it was true. And I knew that together, we could face anything.

"Zo," I said, cutting into her explanation of how we could catch Gloria in the act. "I have an idea. What if we joined forces?"

She blinked, looking confused. "What do you mean? We're already working together on this."

I shook my head, excitement building as the idea took shape. "No, I mean really join forces. What if we combined our businesses?"

Zofia's eyes widened. "You mean like a partnership?"

I nodded enthusiastically. "Exactly. Think about it. Your pottery, my baked goods. We could create gift sets, host events together. We'd be stronger together than we ever could be apart."

For a moment, Zofia was silent, and I felt a flicker of doubt. Had I overstepped? Was this too much, too soon?

But then a slow smile spread across her face. "Corbin Carmichael, you're a genius."

Relief and joy flooded through me. "So you like the idea?"

She laughed, the sound like music to my ears. "Like it? I love it! It's perfect!"

Without thinking, I pulled her into a hug, lifting her off her feet and spinning her around. When I set her down, our faces were inches apart, and I could see every fleck of gold in her hazel eyes.

"Zo," I said softly, my heart pounding. "I need to tell you something."

She looked up at me, her expression a mix of hope and nervousness. "What is it?"

I took a deep breath, gathering my courage. "I love you. I think I have for a while now, but with everything that's happened today, I just couldn't keep it in anymore. You don't have to say it back or anything, I just needed you to know."

For a heart-stopping moment, Zofia was silent. Then, to my amazement, she laughed.

"Corbin, you idiot," she said, her eyes shining with tears. "I love you too."

And then she was kissing me, and the world fell away. All the stress and fear of the day melted into nothing, and all that mattered was Zofia in my arms.

When we finally broke apart, both a little breathless, I rested my forehead against hers. "So, partners in business and in life?"

She grinned, her nose crinkling in that way I loved. "Absolutely."

But even as I reveled in the moment, a nagging worry tugged at the back of my mind. We still had to deal with Gloria and her smear campaign. And something told me she wouldn't go down without a fight.

The next morning, I woke up early, my mind already racing with plans for the day ahead. Zofia and I had stayed up late into the night, strategizing on how to deal with Gloria and her rumors. We'd decided on a two-pronged approach: gather evidence of her wrongdoing while simultaneously launching a positive PR campaign for both our businesses.

I headed downstairs to the bakery, determined to get a head start on the day's baking. As I mixed dough and shaped pastries, I smiled, thinking about Zofia and our newfound partnership, both personal and professional.

Just as I was sliding a tray of croissants into the oven, the bell above the door chimed. I looked up, surprised to see customers so early, only to find myself face to face with Gloria Simmons herself.

"Well, well," she said, her voice dripping with false sweetness. "If it isn't Corbin Carmichael. Hard at work, I see. Though I have to wonder why you bother, given the rumors going around town."

I straightened up, wiping my hands on my apron. "Gloria. To what do I owe the pleasure?"

She sauntered in, running a perfectly manicured finger along the counter. "Oh, I was just in the neighborhood and thought I'd stop by. See how you're holding up under all this unpleasantness."

I clenched my jaw, fighting to keep my temper in check. "We're doing just fine, thanks for your concern. Now, if you'll excuse me, I have work to do."

Gloria's eyes narrowed. "Come now, Corbin. There's no need to be hostile. I'm only trying to help. After all, it must be so difficult, trying to run a business with such a tarnished reputation. Perhaps it's time to consider other options."

I raised an eyebrow. "Other options?"

She nodded, a predatory smile spreading across her face. "I might be willing to take this place off your hands. For a fair price, of course. It would save you the trouble of trying to salvage your reputation."

Anger boiled up inside me, but I forced it down. This

was exactly the evidence we needed. "That's very generous of you, Gloria. But I think we'll manage just fine on our own."

Her smile faltered for a moment before returning full force. "Suit yourself. But don't say I didn't offer when things get worse. And they will get worse, Corbin. Count on it."

With that, she turned on her heel and sauntered out with the bell chiming ominously in her wake.

I let out a breath I didn't realize I'd been holding, my hands shaking slightly. I needed to call Zofia.

An hour later, Zofia burst into the bakery, her cheeks flushed from the chilly November air. "I got here as fast as I could," she said, slightly out of breath. "Are you okay? What exactly did Gloria say?"

I recounted my conversation with Gloria, watching as Zofia's expression shifted from concern to anger to determination.

"This is good," she said when I finished. "We can use this. It's not concrete proof, but it's a start."

I nodded, feeling a renewed sense of purpose. "You're right. And I've been thinking, we need to get ahead of whatever she's planning next."

Zofia's eyes lit up. "The open house! We could move it up, make it a joint event for both our businesses."

"Exactly," I said, grinning. "We'll invite the whole town, show them firsthand that there's nothing to these rumors."

We spent the rest of the morning planning, our excitement growing with each new idea. By lunchtime, we had a solid plan in place. The open house would be this weekend, featuring pottery demonstrations from Zofia, baking workshops from me, and plenty of opportunities for the townspeople to see our processes and ask questions.

As we worked, I realized how in sync we were. Every

time I had an idea, Zofia was right there with a suggestion to make it even better. It felt like we'd been working together for years, not just a few months.

"You know," I said as we took a break for lunch, sharing a plate of sandwiches I'd whipped up, "I think Gloria might have done us a favor."

Zofia looked at me like I'd grown a second head. "How do you figure that?"

I grinned, taking her hand across the table. "Well, if it wasn't for her underhanded tactics, we might never have realized how well we work together. How much stronger we are as a team."

A slow smile spread across Zofia's face. "You're right. And now we have the perfect opportunity to show everyone else, too."

As the day wore on, we split up to tackle our respective tasks. Zofia headed back to her studio to prepare for the pottery demonstrations while I stayed at the bakery, working on recipes for the baking workshops.

Around closing time, just as I was pulling the last batch of sample cookies from the oven, my phone buzzed with a text from Zofia:

You're not going to believe this. Come to the studio ASAP.

My heart raced as I quickly locked up the bakery and jogged down the street to Zofia's studio. What had happened? Had Gloria made another move?

I burst through the door, out of breath, to find Zofia standing by her desk, a strange expression on her face.

"Zo? What's going on?"

She held up a piece of paper. "This was just delivered. It's from the health department."

My stomach dropped. "Oh god, what does it say?"

To my surprise, Zofia broke into a wide grin. "It's a cease and desist order for Gloria's bakery."

I blinked, sure I'd misheard. "What?"

Zofia nodded excitedly. "Apparently, someone tipped them off about some questionable practices at her bakery. They did a surprise inspection this afternoon and found all sorts of violations. She's been shut down pending a full investigation."

A wave of relief washed over me, chased by a twinge of guilt. "Do you think we should feel bad about this?"

Zofia shook her head. "We didn't do anything wrong. We just stood our ground and let the truth come out. Gloria did this to herself."

I nodded, pulling Zofia into a hug. "You're right. And now we can focus on making our businesses even better, together."

As we stood there, wrapped in each other's arms, a sense of peace settled over me. We'd faced our first major challenge as a couple and as business partners, and we'd come out stronger for it.

But even as I reveled in our victory, a small voice in the back of my mind whispered a warning. Gloria might be down, but was she really out? And what other challenges might wait for us just around the corner?

CHAPTER SEVEN

$\mathcal{Z}$ofia

I stood in front of the mirror, adjusting my apron for what felt like the hundredth time that morning. Our new logo, a stylized pottery wheel intertwined with a rolling pin, embroidered the crisp white fabric. It was perfect, just like everything else about this day was going to be perfect. It had to be.

"Zo?" Corbin's voice called from the front of the store. "You ready? People are starting to line up outside."

I took a deep breath, smoothing down my hair one last time. "Coming!" I called back, my voice only slightly shaky.

As I stepped out of the back room and into our new joint storefront, my breath caught in my throat. The space we'd spent weeks renovating looked even more beautiful than I'd imagined. Shelves lined the walls, filled with my pottery creations interspersed with Corbin's artisanal breads and pastries. The center of the store housed a demonstration area where we'd be showcasing our crafts throughout the day.

Corbin stood by the front door, looking unfairly handsome in his matching apron. When he saw me, his face broke into that heart-stopping grin that never failed to make my knees weak.

"There you are," he said, crossing the room to meet me. He placed his hands on my shoulders, his touch instantly calming my nerves. "You look beautiful."

A blush crept up my cheeks. Even after months of dating, he still had that effect on me. "You don't look so bad yourself, Baker Boy."

He laughed, leaning in to press a quick kiss to my forehead. "Ready to make history?"

I nodded, feeling a surge of confidence. "Let's do this."

Together, we walked to the front door. Through the glass, I could see a crowd had gathered - familiar faces from around town, all chatting excitedly. My heart swelled with gratitude for our little community.

Corbin squeezed my hand. "On three?"

I nodded, and we counted together. "One... two... three!"

We threw open the doors, and a cheer went up from the crowd. "Welcome to Kneaded Creations!" we announced in unison, the name we'd chosen after weeks of playful debate.

The next few hours passed in a blur of handshakes, hugs, and heartfelt congratulations. It seemed like the entire town of Wintervale had turned out to support us. Mrs. Pendleton, who had once been so quick to believe the rumors about my pottery, was now gushing over a set of flower-patterned mugs. Mr. Johnson, the high school principal, was sampling Corbin's sourdough with obvious delight.

As the morning wore on, I sat at the pottery wheel, demonstrating my craft to a rapt audience. I loved the feeling of the clay beneath my hands, the way it responded to my touch, transforming from a shapeless lump into something beautiful and useful.

"And that's how you throw a basic bowl," I said, lifting the finished piece off the wheel. "Any questions?"

A young girl in the front raised her hand shyly. "Can I try?"

I smiled, remembering my childhood fascination with pottery. "Of course! Come on up."

As I guided the girl's hands on the wheel, I caught Corbin's eye across the room. He was in the middle of a baking demonstration, his hands covered in flour as he kneaded dough. He winked at me, and I felt a rush of affection so strong it almost took my breath away.

Just then, the bell above the door chimed, and I looked up to see a woman enter. She looked familiar, with the same sandy brown hair and warm eyes as Corbin. My heart skipped a beat as I realized who it must be, Corbin's estranged sister, Emily.

I watched as Corbin froze, his hands stilling in the dough. For a moment, the siblings just stared at each other, and I held my breath, unsure of what would happen next.

Then, to my relief, Corbin's face broke into a tentative smile. "Em," he said, his voice thick with emotion. "You came."

Emily nodded, her eyes shining with unshed tears. "Wouldn't miss it for the world, little brother."

As they embraced, flour and all, my eyes welled up. I knew how much Corbin had been hurting over their estrangement, how much he'd wanted to make things right but hadn't known how.

The rest of the day passed in a whirlwind of activity. Corbin and I tag-teamed demonstrations, served samples, and rang up sales. It was exhausting but exhilarating. Every time I caught Corbin's eye across the room, or felt his hand on the small of my back as he passed by, I felt a thrill of excitement. We were really doing this - not just running a business together, but building a life.

As the sun set, casting a warm glow through the front windows, the crowd finally thinned. Emily, who had stayed to help, was chatting with the last few stragglers.

Corbin came up behind me, wrapping his arms around my waist and resting his chin on my shoulder. "We did it, Zo," he murmured. "We actually did it."

I leaned back into his embrace, feeling a sense of contentment wash over me. "We sure did."

After the last customer left and we'd locked up for the night, Corbin pulled out a bottle of champagne he'd been hiding in the back room. "I think this calls for a celebration," he said with a grin.

We settled onto the floor behind the counter, legs crossed like kids at a picnic. Emily joined us, and as we sipped champagne from pottery mugs (of course), the siblings talked, really talk, for the first time in years.

I listened, offering support when needed, but mostly just witnessing this moment of healing. Corbin opened up about feeling trapped by family expectations, while Emily admitted to her own fears and insecurities that had driven her away. There were tears, but also laughter, and by the end of the night, I could see the bond between them strengthening.

As Emily prepared to leave, she hugged me tightly. "Thank you," she whispered. "For loving my brother, for bringing him back to himself. I've never seen him this happy."

My eyes teared up again. "He makes me happy too," I said simply.

After Emily left, Corbin and I did a final walkthrough of the store, marveling at how different it looked now compared to just that morning. Every empty shelf space, every crumb on the floor, was evidence of our success.

"I still can't quite believe it," I said, running my hand along the smooth wood of the counter. "This is ours."

Corbin came up behind me, wrapping his arms around my waist. "Believe it, beautiful. We made this happen."

I turned in his arms, looking up into those warm brown eyes I loved so much. "We make a pretty good team, don't we?"

He grinned, leaning down to press his forehead against mine. "The best."

As we stood there, wrapped in each other's arms in the quiet of our new store, I felt a sense of peace settle over me. The journey to get here hadn't been easy. We'd faced rumors, sabotage, and our own fears and insecurities. But we'd come through it all stronger, together.

"Corbin," I said softly, my heart suddenly racing. "I love you. So much."

His eyes softened, and he cupped my face in his hands. "I love you too, Zo. More than I ever thought possible."

As he leaned in to kiss me, slow and sweet and full of promise, I felt like my heart might burst with happiness. This was everything I'd ever wanted, everything I'd been afraid to hope for after Marcus.

Later, we relaxed on the small couch we'd put in the break room.

"What are you thinking about?" Corbin asked, his fingers running through my hair.

I turned to him. "Just everything. How much has changed in the past year. How happy I am."

He smiled, tucking a strand of hair behind my ear. "Me

too. You know, when I first saw you in that farmers' market, covered in clay and looking like you wanted to murder your pottery wheel, I never imagined we'd end up here."

I laughed, remembering that day. "Oh god, I was a mess. I can't believe you even talked to me."

"Are you kidding? You were the most beautiful thing I'd ever seen." His voice was soft, sincere, and I felt my heart melt all over again.

"Even with clay in my hair and glaze all over my clothes?" I teased.

He nodded solemnly. "Especially then. I thought, *Now there's a woman who's passionate about what she does.* I knew I had to spend time with you."

I leaned over to kiss him, overcome with love for this man who saw the best in me even when I couldn't see it myself.

As we sat there in the quiet of our new store, I thought about the future. There were still challenges ahead, I knew. Running a business together while navigating a romantic relationship wouldn't always be easy. And there was still so much to learn, so much room to grow.

"Hey," I said, a thought suddenly occurring to me. "We never did decide on a staff photo for the website."

Corbin grinned, reaching for his phone. "No time like the present."

We arranged ourselves on the couch, trying to look at least somewhat professional. Corbin held out his phone, and we smiled at the camera.

"To new beginnings," he said.

"To us," I replied.

The camera flashed, capturing this moment of joy, of love, of new beginnings. As I looked at the photo, I couldn't help but smile. We looked happy, a little disheveled, but undeniably in love.

It was perfect.

As we finally prepared to leave for the night, locking up our new store and stepping out into the cool November air, a sense of anticipation rushed through me. Tomorrow would bring new challenges, new opportunities, new chances to grow and learn together.

Corbin took my hand as we walked to his truck, and I leaned into him, savoring his warmth.

"You know," he said thoughtfully, "I've been thinking about expanding our product line. What do you think about pottery baking dishes? We could combine our skills, create something truly unique."

A spark of excitement inspired me at the idea. "That could be amazing. We could do an entire line of oven-to-table pieces."

He grinned, pulling me closer. "See? This is why we make such a great team."

As we drove home, the streets of Wintervale were quiet and peaceful around us, I thought about all the possibilities that lay ahead. New products, new techniques, maybe even classes where we could teach both pottery and baking.

But more than that, I was excited about the life we were building together. The quiet moments in the morning, sharing coffee before we opened the store. The inside jokes that would develop as we worked side-by-side day after day. The challenges we'd face and overcome together.

As we drove home that night, everything fell into place. The store's grand opening had been a smashing success. Corbin had reconnected with his sister, and our relationship was stronger than ever. It felt like we were on the cusp of something truly magical.

The next few weeks flew by in a whirlwind of activity.

We settled into a rhythm at the store, learning to balance our individual crafts with our new joint venture. Corbin's idea for pottery baking dishes turned out to be a hit, and we spent many late nights experimenting with designs and glazes that could withstand oven temperatures.

Before I knew it, Christmas was upon us. Wintervale transformed into a winter wonderland, with twinkling lights adorning every storefront and a thick blanket of snow covering the ground. Our store window featured a display of festive pottery filled with Corbin's holiday-themed treats, drawing in customers like moths to a flame.

On Christmas Eve, Corbin insisted on closing the store early. "We've been working non-stop for weeks," he said, his eyes twinkling with mischief. "I think we deserve a little Christmas magic of our own, don't you?"

I laughed, feeling a flutter of excitement in my stomach. "What did you have in mind, Baker Boy?"

He grinned, pulling me close. "It's a surprise. Just dress warm and meet me back here at seven, okay?"

Intrigued, I agreed. I spent the next few hours at home, trying on and discarding outfits like a teenager before a first date. I finally settled on a cozy sweater dress in deep burgundy, paired with thick leggings and my favorite boots.

When I arrived back at the store, my breath caught in my throat. Corbin had transformed the front display into a winter wonderland. Twinkling fairy lights hung everywhere, casting a warm glow over a picnic blanket spread out on the floor. A wicker basket sat in the center, and I could smell the enticing aroma of fresh bread and spices.

"Corbin?" I called out, my voice soft with wonder.

He appeared from the back room, looking devastatingly handsome in a crisp button-down and slacks. "Surprise," he said, his smile a little nervous. "Do you like it?"

I threw my arms around him, overwhelmed with love. "It's perfect," I whispered against his neck.

We settled onto the blanket, and Corbin began unpacking the basket. There was a thermos of hot mulled wine, a loaf of his famous cranberry walnut bread, and an assortment of cheeses and fruits. As we ate and talked, watching the snow fall gently outside, a sense of peace and contentment washed over me.

After we'd finished eating, Corbin cleared his throat, suddenly looking nervous again. "Zo," he said, taking my hands in his. "This past year has been the best of my life. Meeting you, falling in love with you, building this business together is more than I ever dreamed possible."

My heart raced as I realized where this might be going. "Corbin..."

He smiled, reaching into his pocket. "Zofia Nowak, you are the most incredible woman I've ever known. You're talented, kind, stubborn as hell sometimes." I laughed at that, feeling tears prick at my eyes. "And I can't imagine spending a single day without you for the rest of my life."

He pulled out a small velvet box and opened it, revealing a stunning ring. The center stone was a deep blue sapphire, surrounded by tiny diamonds that sparkled in the fairy lights. "Will you marry me?"

For a moment, I couldn't speak. My mind flashed back to Marcus, to the fear and doubt that had plagued me for so long. But looking into Corbin's eyes, seeing the love and sincerity there, I knew this was different. This was real.

"Yes," I whispered, then louder, "Yes! Of course, I'll marry you!"

Corbin's face broke into the biggest grin I'd ever seen as he slipped the ring onto my finger. Then he was pulling me into his arms, kissing me with a passion that left me breathless.

When we finally broke apart, both of us laughing and crying a little, I couldn't stop staring at the ring on my finger. "It's beautiful," I said. "How did you know?"

Corbin looked a little sheepish. "I may have had some help from Emily. And your mom."

I gasped. "You talked to my mom?"

He nodded. "I wanted to do this right. I called her last week to ask for her blessing. She cried, by the way. Said she's never heard you sound so happy as when you talk about me."

Fresh tears sprang to my eyes. "I love you so much," I said, pulling him in for another kiss.

The next few months passed in a blur of wedding planning and running the store. We decided on a June wedding, wanting to take advantage of the beautiful Wintervale summer. My mom flew in from Poland to help with the preparations, and it touched me by how well she and Corbin bonded. She kept calling him her *syn*, her son, which never failed to make him blush.

Emily proved to be an invaluable help, throwing herself into wedding planning with gusto. It was wonderful to see the bond between the siblings growing stronger every day. Even Corbin's parents, who had initially been skeptical about our whirlwind romance and business partnership, came around. Mr. Carmichael even offered to bake our wedding cake, a gesture that brought tears to Corbin's eyes.

*B*efore I knew it, June had arrived, and I stood in front of a mirror in the bridal suite of the Wintervale Botanical Gardens. My dress was simple but elegant, a flowing A-line gown with delicate lace details. I swept my hair up in a loose updo, with tendrils framing my face.

"Oh, kochanie," my mom said, her eyes welling up with tears. "You look so beautiful."

Emily, stunning in her maid of honor dress, nodded in agreement. "Corbin's not going to know what hit him."

I took a deep breath, trying to calm the butterflies in my stomach. "I can't believe this is really happening," I said, my voice barely above a whisper.

Just then, there was a knock at the door. Emily opened it to reveal Corbin's dad, looking dapper in a suit. "It's time," he said with a warm smile.

As the music started and I began my walk down the aisle, my eyes locked with Corbin's. He looked impossibly handsome in his dark blue suit, but it was the look of pure love and adoration on his face that took my breath away. At that moment, all my nerves disappeared. This was right. This was where I was meant to be.

The ceremony passed in a blur of happy tears and heartfelt vows. When the officiant finally pronounced us husband and wife, Corbin pulled me into a kiss that made me forget about everyone else in the room. The cheers and applause from our friends and family barely registered as I lost myself in the moment.

The reception was everything we'd hoped for and more. We held it in a beautifully restored barn just outside of town in an apple orchard, decorated with fairy lights and wildflowers. We set the tables with my handmade pottery, filled with Corbin's artisanal breads and local cheeses.

Our first dance was to "Can't Help Falling in Love," and as Corbin twirled me around the dance floor, I felt like I was floating on air. "Have I told you how beautiful you look, Mrs. Carmichael?" he whispered in my ear.

I grinned, still not used to my new name. "You might have mentioned it once or twice, Mr. Carmichael. But feel free to keep saying it."

As the night wore on, a sense of gratitude overwhelmed me. Looking around at our friends and family, all laughing and dancing and celebrating our love, I couldn't believe how lucky I was. From the couple who had bought the first piece of pottery from our joint store, to my old art school friends who had flown in from across the country, to Corbin's extended family who had welcomed me with open arms, and everyone who had touched our lives was here to share in our joy.

Later, as we said goodbye to the last of our guests and prepared to leave for our honeymoon, Corbin pulled me aside. "I have one more surprise for you," he said, his eyes twinkling.

"Corbin, you've already given me everything I could ever want," I protested, but he just shook his head.

"Close your eyes," he instructed. I did as he asked, feeling him slip something into my hands. "Okay, open them."

I looked down to see a small, beautifully glazed pottery box. With trembling hands, I opened it to find a key inside. "What's this?" I asked, confused.

Corbin's smile was soft and full of love. "It's the key to our new home. I found this little cottage just outside of town. It's got plenty of room for a home studio for you, and a big kitchen for me. And..." he paused, suddenly looking a little nervous, "maybe someday, room for a nursery?"

Tears sprang to my eyes as I threw my arms around him. "It's perfect," I whispered. "You're perfect."

As we drove away from the reception, waving goodbye to our loved ones, I couldn't stop smiling. The future stretched out before us, full of possibilities. I knew there would be challenges ahead with running a business together, navigating married life, maybe even starting a family one day.

Our honeymoon was a blissful two weeks in Greece, split between the historic streets of Athens and a quiet villa on Santorini. We explored ancient ruins, swam in crystal-clear waters, and ate our weight in fresh seafood and baklava. But more than anything, we just enjoyed being together, reveling in our new status as husband and wife.

One evening, as we sat on our villa's balcony watching the sunset paint the white-washed buildings in shades of pink and gold, Corbin turned to me with a thoughtful expression. "You know," he said, "I've been thinking about something."

I raised an eyebrow, amused. "Uh oh. Should I be worried?"

He laughed, pulling me closer. "No, nothing like that. I was just thinking about how we could expand the business when we get back."

I nestled into his side, intrigued. "What did you have in mind?"

"Well," he said, his eyes lighting up with excitement, "what if we started offering classes? You could teach pottery, I could do baking workshops. We could even do some joint classes, combining both our skills."

A spark of excitement flourished in my mind at the idea. "That could be amazing. We could reach a whole new customer base, maybe even draw in tourists looking for a unique experience."

Corbin nodded enthusiastically. "Exactly! And it would be a great way to connect more with the community, share our passions with others."

As we continued to brainstorm ideas, I marveled at how in sync we were. Even on our honeymoon, we couldn't help but dream up new ways to grow our shared vision. But it didn't feel like work. It was just another way we expressed our love and partnership.

When we returned to Wintervale, bronzed and relaxed from our time in the Mediterranean, we threw ourselves into implementing our new ideas. We converted part of the store into a teaching space, and within a few months, our classes were consistently selling out.

Our new cottage quickly became home, filled with a mix of my pottery creations and Corbin's baking experiments. We spent our evenings curled up on the porch swing, talking about our days and dreaming about the future. It wasn't always perfect because we had our share of disagreements and stressful days at the store, but we always came back to each other, stronger for having worked through our challenges together.

As summer faded into fall, I reflected on how much had changed in just over a year. From that first farmers' market where I'd been ready to throw in the towel, to now being married to the love of my life, running a successful business, and happier than I'd ever been.

One crisp October morning, as I stood at my potter's wheel in our home studio, a wave of nausea washed over me. I'd been feeling off for a few days, but had chalked it up to a busy schedule at the store. But now, as I counted back in my head, I realized I was late. Very late.

With shaking hands, I pulled out the pregnancy test I'd bought on a whim the week before, just in case. Five minutes later, I was staring at two pink lines, my heart pounding in my chest.

When Corbin came home that evening, I was waiting for him on the porch swing, a small gift box in my lap. "What's this?" he asked, his face lighting up like a kid at Christmas.

"Open it," I said, trying to keep my voice steady.

He untied the ribbon and lifted the lid, revealing a tiny pair of baby booties I'd made from clay. For a moment, he just stared, uncomprehending. Then his eyes snapped to mine, wide with shock and hope. "Zo... are you...?"

I nodded, tears spilling down my cheeks. "We're going to have a baby."

The joy on Corbin's face was indescribable. He swept me up in his arms, spinning me around as we both laughed and cried. "I love you," he kept saying, over and over. "I love you so much."

As we stood there on our porch, wrapped in each other's arms with the setting sun painting the sky in brilliant hues, I felt a sense of completeness wash over me. This was everything I'd ever wanted, everything I'd been afraid to hope for after the heartbreak with Marcus.

Corbin placed a gentle hand on my still-flat stomach, his eyes filled with wonder. "I can't believe we're going to be parents," he said softly.

I covered his hand with mine, feeling a surge of love for this man who had changed my life in so many ways. "We're going to be great parents," I said, surprising myself with how much I believed it.

As we went inside, already talking about nursery designs and baby names, I couldn't help but marvel at the journey that had brought us here. From two strangers at a farmers' market to partners in every sense of the word, our love story had been one of growth, trust, and the courage to open our hearts.

I knew that the road ahead wouldn't always be easy. Balancing a new baby with our business would be a challenge, and we still had so much to learn about parenthood. But as I looked at Corbin, saw the love and excitement shining in his eyes, I knew we could handle anything life threw our way.

Corbin and Zofia announce the birth of their baby daughter, Ella
Lousie, born on their 1 year anniversary.

This was our happily ever after, not an ending, but the beginning of a whole new adventure. And I couldn't wait to see where it would take us next.

Read the next cozy autumn romance: Apples and Clay.

ABOUT ANN LAUREL

Ann loves writing about life and issues Christian couples face, all with a big dose of romance.

Sign up for Ann's newsletter.

Printed in Dunstable, United Kingdom